My Magical Pony

Sea Haze

The **My Magical Pony** series:

Other series by Jenny Oldfield:

Sea Haze

By Jenny Oldfield

Illustrated by Gillian Martin

Hodder
Children's
Books

A division of Hodder Headline Limited

To the real Molly – every bit as gorgeous!

Text copyright © 2006 Jenny Oldfield
Illustrations copyright © 2006 Gillian Martin

First published in Great Britain in 2006
by Hodder Children's Books

The rights of Jenny Oldfield and Gillian Martin to be identified as the
Author and Illustrator of the Work respectively have been asserted by them in
accordance with the Copyright, Designs and Patents Act 1988.

1

A Catalogue record for this book is available from the British Library

ISBN-10: 0 340 91842 X
ISBN-13: 9780340918425

Printed and bound in Great Britain by
Bookmarque Ltd, Croydon, Surrey

The paper and board used in this paperback by Hodder Children's Books are
natural recyclable products made from wood grown in sustainable forests. The
manufacturing processes conform to the environmental
regulations of the country of origin.

Hodder Children's Books
A division of Hodder Headline Limited
338 Euston Road, London NW1 3BH

Chapter One

A mist blew in from the sea. Krista could hardly see where they were going, but she trusted Shining Star to get them off the shore on to safe ground.

"Hold tight!" her magical pony told her.

Krista felt him spread his wide, white wings and beat them. Gently they rose from the ground in a silver shining cloud. "Follow us!" she said to the shadowy group of wild ponies half hidden by the mist.

The bedraggled ponies stumbled along the pebble beach. They had almost drowned,

blocked by the high tide in a narrow inlet and unable to see which way to go until Krista and Shining Star had come to the rescue.

"This way!" Star called out, hovering over the sharp headland of Black Point, watching as the ponies carefully picked their way.

From the safety of his broad back, Krista saw the mighty waves crash and break on to the dark rocks. His beating wings blew her dark hair from her face, the damp mist clung to her cheeks. *Thank heavens he came!* she said to herself. *Without his magic, these ponies would have died!*

Now though they followed Star's glowing light, the high tide pushing them ever on and up on to higher ground along the path that Krista's magical pony had discovered. Soon

they were out of reach of the dangerous waves.

"Thank you, Star, you're brilliant!" Krista
waited for him to land then slipped from his
back. She reached up and stroked his silky
smooth neck and mane.

He lowered his head to nudge her gently
with his nose. "You must take some of the
praise," he reminded her. "If you had not
spotted the ponies at Black Point and called for
me, there would have been no happy ending."

My Magical Pony

She smiled back at him. "We're a team!"

"And look, the wild ponies know who to thank!" Star went on.

Krista turned to see the stocky little ponies approach her. They were wet and breathing hard, their dark manes tangled.

"Hey, how tame are you!" she murmured, counting six ponies – some grey, some chestnut, all shaggy and unshod. "You're supposed to be wild!"

But they came close, nuzzling at her and Shining Star.

Krista stroked them each in turn. "You're gorgeous!" she told them, sorry when they turned away at last and prepared to head up the long grassy slope towards Hartfell Moor.

Sea Haze

Shining Star spoke briefly to the sturdy chestnut mare who seemed to be the leader of the group. "We wish you well and bid you farewell," he said solemnly.

The mare tossed her head then broke into a trot up the hill. The others followed.

"And I must say goodbye to you too," Shining Star told Krista. "I will fly home to Galishe then rest."

"Me too." Before the rescue, Krista had worked all day at Jo Weston's stables, helping with the ponies and trekking along Whitton Sands. Now she was ready for bed. "Only, I guess I won't be *flying* home!" she laughed.

"Think of me in the night sky," the magical pony said gently.

"Amongst the stars!" Krista's eyes shone. Then she suddenly remembered a reason why she must hurry on. "Oops, I'm supposed to be meeting Darcy Stevens and Molly at eight o'clock!" she gasped.

"Then goodbye," Star said, spreading his wings. He scattered silver dust as he rose into the air.

Looking up, Krista felt the magic dust land on her face and bare arms, making them glitter.

Shining Star beat his wings more rapidly, rising high into the evening sky where the low sun shone bright red and gold.

"Thank you, Star!" Krista whispered. She waited a few moments to see him fly over the wide bay towards the setting sun. "Goodbye!"

Sea Haze

*

The perfect end to a perfect day. Though she was tired, Krista ran along the cliff path to make it home before eight. She was glad when High Point Farm came into sight, perched high on the moorside, sheltered by tall trees.

My Magical Pony

Her house looked cosy in the golden rays, with its long, sloping roof and tiny windows, a garden to two sides, plus a neat yard where her dad parked his car and her mum grew bright flowers in old stone troughs.

Krista jogged on, watching a car drive up the lane towards the house, knowing that it would be Darcy and her mum, with Molly their gorgeous golden retriever. The visitors would arrive just before her.

Cool day! she thought. *First I get to groom Comanche, Misty and Shandy. Then I ride out on Kiki. Finally my magical pony comes to help me lead the wild ponies off Black Point. Now I get to meet Molly. What could be better?*

*

12

Sea Haze

"Hi, Krista!" Darcy stood on the stile at the end of the cliff path. She waved both arms and yelled at the top of her voice.

Krista arrived out of breath. "Sorry I'm late. Where's Molly?"

"In the front garden with Mum. Your mum said you wouldn't be long."

Krista nodded. "Cool. Have you packed your bags?"

"Yeah, we have to be ready to set off before breakfast tomorrow. We fly out at ten." Darcy was excited by the visit to Disney that the family had in store, but she was sad to leave Molly. "I'm glad you're looking after her," she admitted to Krista.

"I'm glad too!" Together Krista and Darcy

13

crossed the lane then skirted round the side of
the house into the front garden. There the
two mums sat chatting in the late sun.

"Where's Molly?" Darcy called.

"Last seen poking about in the hedge
bottom." Mrs Stevens pointed them in the
right direction and the girls ran to the spot.

Darcy crouched down by the green
hawthorn bushes. "Here, Moll!" she called.

"Uh-oh, I've a feeling she's on Spike's trail,"
Krista guessed. Spike was her pet hedgehog,
and he had lots of sharp bristles that Molly
might not like!

There was a rustling on the far side of the
hedge, but still no Molly.

"Molly, come here!" Darcy insisted.

Sea Haze

The rustling grew louder then there was a sharp, surprised yelp.

"Whoops!" Krista grimaced. It sounded like Molly had found Spike.

Sure enough, a sad face appeared through the undergrowth. There was a pair of large brown eyes, a lot of creamy fur, a black nose and two floppy ears.

Darcy tutted. "Molly, what have you done?" she murmured.

Hanging her head, Molly crawled further into view, her long tail between her legs. She went up to Darcy and held out a front paw.

"Aah, did you get a thorn in your foot?"

Krista heard a lighter rustling sound and spotted the culprit trotting rapidly across the lawn. "No, it was probably Spike. Sorry about that," she muttered.

But Darcy shook her head and left Molly to lick her paw. "Not his fault. Anyway, she won't make the same mistake twice. Will you, Moll?"

The dog looked up, her big eyes serious, her ears drooping.

Krista crouched down. "Come here, Molly!" she whispered. She smiled as the golden retriever wearily raised herself and padded towards her, wagging her tail. "I'm Krista – remember me?" she said, stroking the thick, soft fur.

16

Sea Haze

"This is where you're staying while we go on holiday," Darcy explained, looking almost as sad as Molly. "But we'll be back in two weeks, don't worry!"

Molly's tail swished against Krista, who put her arms around the dog's neck. "We'll look after you!" she promised. "We'll give you lovely food and take you on lots of walks."

"Be good!" Darcy told her beloved dog as her mum came to fetch her.

Krista hugged Molly tight. "You can come to the stables with me!" she murmured. "I promise, you're going to love it!"

Chapter Two

Molly's bed fitted nicely in the hallway at the bottom of the stairs. Her two bowls – one for water, one for food – were by the kitchen door.

"Here's your special blanket," Krista told her, folding it then tucking it into the basket. It was time for bed. "All lovely and cosy!"

Molly padded through the house, sniffing here and snuffling there.

"Whoa!" Krista's dad cried, not seeing the visitor and almost tripping over her.

"Dad, watch where you're going!" Krista protested. "Molly's quite old and doddery.

Sea Haze

In fact, she's older than Darcy, so she doesn't want you falling over her!"

"Never mind her – *I'm* quite old and doddery!" he laughed. He could see that Krista would treat Molly like royalty for the two weeks of her stay. "She's going to get far better treatment than me. In fact, I'm thinking of sleeping downstairs in *her* bed!"

"Oh no you don't!" Quickly Krista called Molly to her and settled her down for the night with a long stroke and some murmured words. "I know you're missing Darcy! But she's gone on a lovely holiday, and you're going to have the *best* time here with us!"

Molly lay down on her soft red blanket

and sighed. She curled her tail beneath her and rested her head.

"There!" Krista watched and was satisfied. Soon Molly's eyes began to close.

"Time for your bed too," Krista's mum reminded her, passing by with armfuls of laundry.

Sea Haze

Krista gave Molly one last stroke. "Goodnight!" she whispered, going upstairs and changing into her pyjamas.

She washed her face, brushed hair and teeth, opened her curtains so that she could stare out at the night sky. Then she slid under her duvet.

The sheets were cool and clean. *Hmm – not tired!* she thought, looking out at the moon. *Too excited!*

She pictured herself cycling along the cliff path with Molly at her heels, mucking out at the stables while Molly sat and watched. She saw them riding out on Whitton Sands, where Molly would fetch sticks and race into the waves. She would swim then scamper out and shake herself dry.

21

My Magical Pony

"I've always wanted a dog!" she sighed. "And now I have one, even if it's only for two weeks!"

Outside the window, stars twinkled. Shining Star looked down from Galishe at Krista gazing into space. "All is well," he told himself. He folded his wings and slept.

Next morning Krista was awake early.

She stretched underneath her warm bed-clothes, yawned then suddenly remembered the special guest. She leaped up and ran barefoot downstairs.

Molly was already awake and waiting to greet Krista. She wagged her tail so hard that her sturdy back end swayed to and fro.

Sea Haze

"Hi, Moll!" Krista knelt on the floor beside her. "Did you have a good sleep? Are you ready to come to Hartfell with me?"

The dog waggled and shook with pleasure.

"Can we have a bit of hush down there?" Krista's dad called from the bedroom. "It's six o'clock on Saturday morning. Some of us round here would like a lie-in!"

"Sorry!" Krista called back, giggling at Molly. She led the dog into the kitchen where she ran fresh water into her bowl. "Drink this while I go up and get dressed," she said quietly. "As soon as I've had breakfast we'll set off for the stables."

She left Molly lapping noisily and sped off to put on her clothes. A glance out of the

23

window told her that the weather was
bright but breezy, so she chose jeans, a red
sweatshirt and a denim jacket. Then she ran a
brush through her short dark hair and speedily
brushed her teeth. She was back downstairs
before Molly had finished her drink.

"Breakfast!" she muttered, grabbing a cereal
bar and an apple and stuffing them in her
pocket. She couldn't wait to be out there
cycling along the cliff path with Molly at
her heels.

"OK!" Krista announced, taking Molly's red
lead off a coat hook in the hallway.

But as they opened the back door and
Krista began to unlock the padlock on her
bike, the phone rang.

Sea Haze

Krista checked her watch – 6.25. She
dashed back inside to find her bleary-eyed
dad already answering the phone. "It's for
you!" he muttered when he saw Krista, and he
handed her the phone.

"Hi Krista, it's me, Darcy!"

"Darcy, hi! What time do
you call this? Are you at the
airport?"

"Yep. Listen, we're boarding
the plane in half an hour. I just
wanted to know how Molly is
before we set off."

"Molly's fine!" Krista raised her eyebrows at
her dad as he turned and stumbled wearily
back to bed.

My Magical Pony

"Are you sure? How's her sore paw?"

"Totally better. She slept right through the night and she's here now looking up at me and wagging her tail as we speak." Krista leaned down and put the phone close to the dog's mouth. "Say hello to Darcy, Molly!"

Woof! Molly gave a throaty bark.

"See!" Krista said into the phone. "She's cool!"

There was a pause on the other end. "So she isn't missing me?" Darcy asked.

Krista smiled to herself. "Yeah, she's pining for you. She won't eat, she won't drink, she just sits at the door waiting for you to come back! No, not really! Listen, Darcy, just get on the plane and have a cool time.

26

Molly and me will be OK."

Darcy sniffed back the tears. "And you'll look after her for me and not let anything bad happen to her?"

For a moment Krista was serious. "I promise!"

"Thanks, Krista!" Darcy sounded brighter. "You're a really good mate."

"No problem," Krista replied. "Now relax and go get on that plane."

"Say bye to Molly for me," Darcy begged.

Enough already! "OK, OK, now scram!" Krista said and quickly put down the phone.

"What a cute dog!" Carrie Jordan said, making a big fuss of Molly in the yard at Hartfell.

"Never even knew you had one," Nathan

27

Steele said to Krista, who was mucking out Kiki's empty stable.

"Molly's not mine," Krista explained. "I'm looking after her while her owner's away."

Nathan went over to stroke Molly. "How old is she?" he asked.

"Eleven, I think. But she still runs around and plays with a stick. No way does she act her age."

As if to prove it, Molly spotted one of Jo Weston's black cats creeping down the side of the long tack room. She woofed and bounded towards it, skidding to a halt as the cat vanished round the corner.

"Cat alert!" Carrie grinned. "It's like a cartoon – dog sees cat. Dog chases cat!"

28

Sea Haze

"And misses!" Nathan laughed.

Krista came out of the stable and leaned
on her shovel. Then she took off her jacket
and slung it over the stable door. "Hey, am I
the only one who's doing any work around
here?"

Grinning, Nathan and Carrie took up their
brooms and began to sweep the yard before
other riders arrived for their morning trek.

My Magical Pony

Jo came out of the tack room with headcollars and strode off to fetch Shandy and Woody from the field.

"Here, Molly!" Krista called, making sure that the dog didn't follow Jo.

Obediently Molly trotted across and sat patiently outside Kiki's stable while Krista worked on.

"How about Molly coming with us when we trek out?" Krista asked Jo when she returned with the two ponies.

Jo nodded as she led Shandy into her stable. "No problem," she agreed. "She doesn't seem like the sort of dog who would be a nuisance."

As if she understood, Molly trotted up to Jo to receive a pat and a stroke. "You're a bit old

and creaky in the joints, just like Shandy
here," Jo smiled. "And you're a lovely gentle
girl, aren't you?"

Molly wagged her tail and lapped up the
praise. Meanwhile, Krista took a brush and
curry comb into Shandy's stable and began to
groom the pony.

"Look at the mess your mane is in!" she
grumbled quietly. The long, thick hair was
twisted and knotted. "Anyone would think no
one ever brushed it!"

Shandy sighed and stood patiently while
Krista untangled her mane. Her dark brown
coat shone rich as chocolate, and by the time
Krista had finished, her black mane was silky
smooth.

"That's better!" Krista nodded, standing
back to view the end result.

Then Nathan peered over the stable door
and told Krista to get a move on.
"Everybody's here," he reported. "Jo's going to
give Janey a lesson on Drifter. Carrie's riding
Misty. Two people I don't know have asked

Sea Haze

for Kiki and Misty. That leaves Shandy and Woody. Who do you want to ride?"

"I'll take Shandy out," Krista decided. "It's ages since I rode her."

Soon all the ponies were saddled and the group of riders gathered by the mounting block in the yard. Molly stuck close by Krista as she mounted the dark bay pony. "Good girl, stay with me," Krista said.

Jo went around checking girths. "Everybody's hat securely fastened?" she asked. "Krista will lead the trek on Shandy. Where do you all want to go?"

"The moor!" Carrie said.

"The beach!" the newcomers and Nathan chimed in.

My Magical Pony

So the beach it was, and Krista rode out of the yard, across the lane on to the field leading down towards the cliffs. It was a bridleway track that she'd ridden many times before, but it was Molly's first time, so Krista was glad when the dog plodded along steadily by her side.

Behind her, the small group of riders chatted and pointed out small farms tucked into the hillside, some sheep, and once, a small group of wild moorland ponies.

I wonder if those are the ones we rescued from Black Point yesterday, Krista thought, smiling as she recalled Shining Star. "Come on, Moll!" she urged, seeing that Molly had paused to study the far-off ponies grazing amongst the heather.

Sea Haze

Quickly Molly fell in alongside Shandy and they rode on towards the beach.

Once on the sands, the group spread out. "Meet at the far end of the beach in ten minutes!" Krista called, trotting Shandy towards the shallow waves, with faithful Molly following.

Shandy halted at the water's edge.

"Wimp!" Krista laughed, squeezing the pony's sides to urge her on.

But the pony didn't like the look of the cold, foaming water. She tossed her head and stood firm.

It was Molly who went bounding into the waves with a happy bark, frisking and frolicking through the water, then plunging in for a swim.

My Magical Pony

"See!" Krista exclaimed. "That's how it's done!"

Gingerly Shandy put one hoof into the water. She shivered and drew it back.

Krista watched Molly swim strongly, her head just visible above the water. The sun shone on the shallow waves, making them sparkle. Still Shandy refused to step into the sea.

"Never mind!" Krista smiled to herself. She glanced at the other riders galloping their ponies along the sand then called the dog back.

Molly turned and doggy-paddled back to the shore. She waded out, her coat dripping wet, then stood and shook herself dry.

Sea Haze

"Hey!" Krista exclaimed as the glittering droplets showered her and Shandy.

Woof! Molly shook herself some more.

"Let's go!" Krista cried, turning Shandy towards the far end of the beach.

And with Molly at Krista's side, they galloped in the wind.

Chapter Three

"So!" Krista's mum watched Krista brush Molly's coat early next morning. "Which do you like best – ponies or dogs?"

Krista picked loose hair out of the dog brush and piled it carefully on a sheet of newspaper. She thought Spike might like to use it to build his winter nest when the time came. "That's not fair," she replied. "I can't choose. It's the same as me asking you, 'Who do you like best, me or dad!' I love dogs and ponies both the same."

"Good answer," her dad told her with a grin.

Sea Haze

"But if I were you, I'd get out of here before your mum gets chance to argue back. Otherwise you'll be here all day!"

"Are you saying I'm an argumentative type?" Krista's mum protested, picking up a cushion and bashing Krista's dad across the shoulder with it.

He ducked and the cushion caught Molly instead.

Woof! Molly joined in the game, grabbing the cushion and running out into the yard.

"Oops!" Krista pulled a face as the cushion ripped and white feathers floated in the air. "I'm out of here!" she gasped, making a run for it. "Come on, Moll!" she called, disappearing on to the lane with her bike and dog.

My Magical Pony

"OK, so who *do* you like best – Krista or me?" her dad grinned, standing face to face with her mum as Krista and Molly sped along the cliff path.

At Hartfell, Jo was already mucking out and grooming ponies. Her two cats, Lucy and Holly, spotted Molly and made themselves scarce. "Hi Krista!" Jo called. "Glad you're here. We've got a busy day."

So Krista got quickly to work, fetching in the ponies two at a time and starting to groom them while Molly sniffed around the yard.

"Stand!" Krista told Misty, the pretty roan pony whose pale grey coat was flecked pinkish-brown.

Sea Haze

Molly
ambled into
the hay barn
and startled two
pigeons perched in the
rafters. The birds flapped
their wings and flew out of the
high window.

Krista brushed Misty's back and belly then
moved on to groom Shandy.

Out in the yard once more, Molly tried to
sidle up to Lucy and Holly to make friends.
The cats hissed and arched their backs.

"Are you happy to ride Shandy again
today?" Jo asked Krista, wheeling a full
barrow across the yard.

My Magical Pony

Krista nodded, brushing the bay pony's dark coat until it shone. "Cool. Molly really likes her. She runs beside us everywhere we go!"

As if to prove it, Molly trotted up to Shandy and sniffed around her front hooves. The pony lowered her head and nuzzled the dog.

"Can I lead a ride along the bridleway to Mill Lane?" Krista asked.

"Sure, go for it," Jo agreed.

Then riders started to arrive and the ponies had to be tacked up, so that by 9.30 the group was ready to leave. Krista rushed here and there with bridles while Jo carried the saddles out of the tack room.

"Nice day!" Mr Henderson said as he dropped

off his daughter, Alice. The Hendersons kept their own pony, Nessie, here at Hartfell.

Alice shot off to fetch Nessie in from the field. "Wait for me!" she called to Krista, her red ponytail bobbing as she ran. "Don't set off without me!"

Krista was glad to wait – she looked forward to chatting with Alice as they rode along. Since Alice's family had come down from Scotland, Alice and Krista had become good mates.

("Both pony-mad!" their mums agreed. "They live, breathe and sleep ponies!")

"Alice, meet Molly!" Krista said once Alice's grey pony was brought in and safely tethered. "Molly – Alice!"

My Magical Pony

The two said hi with a wagging tail and quick stroke.

"I didn't know you had—" Alice began.

"I don't!" Krista cut in. "She belongs to Darcy Stevens, from school."

"Oh yeah, I know. Are you looking after Molly?" Swiftly Alice put on her pony's bridle and saddle. Jo came and checked the girth. Then Alice tucked her ponytail under her hard hat and fastened the strap. "Ready!" she gasped.

Today there were five other riders, plus Alice and Krista. They headed down the moorside towards Whitton, but turned on to a bridleway before they reached town. The old track wound between tall hedges, with fields to either side.

Sea Haze

"Does this route come out near the old mill?" Alice asked, riding close behind Krista and Shandy. Molly had tucked herself in beside them.

Krista nodded. "We come out on Mill Lane, not far from the house."

Once she knew where they were, Alice hung back to talk to other riders and Krista rode ahead. She ducked to avoid a low branch then yelled a warning to the others.

My Magical Pony

Soon she saw an opening on to a narrow road. "Stay back, Moll," she said, bringing Shandy to a halt at the exit from the bridlepath. She sat still in the saddle, listening and watching for cars on the road.

All was quiet. "OK!" she decided, easing Shandy forward.

All of a sudden a white shape hurtled towards Krista and Shandy. It was a small dog, shooting out of the gateway of the Old Mill, barking and yapping loudly.

"Get back!" Krista yelled, afraid that the little terrier would upset the ponies. Shandy backed away, bunching into Alice and the riders who followed.

Sea Haze

"Where's the owner?" Alice said in a worried voice.

Still the dog raced towards them, snarling and snapping. Shandy's ears went back flat against her head.

"This is not nice!" Krista muttered between gritted teeth. She tried to turn her pony to face the dog as it flew towards them.

"Buster, come here!" A figure appeared at the gate of the old house.

Straight away Krista recognised Holly Owen, a girl from school. "Get back!" she warned the dog again.

My Magical Pony

Buster ignored them both. He flew at Shandy, lips curled back to show two rows of sharp white teeth. Krista felt Shandy rear and threw her weight forward in the saddle to keep her balance. Luckily she stayed on and her pony landed back on all fours.

Now the terrier had reached them and darted under Shandy's belly. He snapped at her legs, darting in and out. Alice and the other riders were now having trouble controlling their own ponies.

"Buster, you're a bad boy!" Holly called feebly from her gateway. "Come here!"

"Whoa!" Alice cried at Nessie, as Shandy quivered and shook. "Why doesn't somebody do something?"

Sea Haze

Suddenly, as if in answer to Alice's question, Molly sprang to life. She leaped out of the narrow bridleway path on to the road, barking and growling at the little terrier. Like a whirlwind she rushed at Buster, her own teeth bared, sounding fierce as a lion.

Yip! The terrier caught sight of the new enemy. He shot out from under Shandy's feet and scuttled down into the ditch at the side of the road to hide. Molly plunged in after him.

"Go, Molly!" Alice and the others shouted, while Krista calmed her pony down.

There was a lot of scuffling, a yelp, and then Buster came back into sight. His white body was covered in mud and he was running away, tail between his legs.

My Magical Pony

"Well done, Molly!" Krista breathed a sigh of relief, seeing Holly Owen take a few steps towards them to pick up her dog.

Molly emerged from the ditch and came trotting up, tail wagging.

"You're a hero!" Alice cried.

"A *heroine!*" Krista corrected.

A grateful Shandy lowered her head to nuzzle Molly.

Meanwhile, Holly began to complain from a distance. "Your dog attacked my poor little Buster!"

"Did you hear that!" Alice's mouth fell open. "How about you keeping your dog on a lead in future? That way it won't race out and spook people's horses!"

Sea Haze

Krista didn't want any
fuss. The main thing was,
everyone was safe. "Ssh!"
she warned Alice. "I'll ask
Jo to phone Holly's mum
when we get back to
Hartfell."

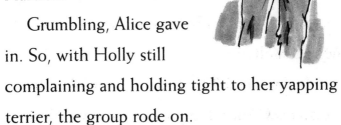

Grumbling, Alice gave
in. So, with Holly still
complaining and holding tight to her yapping
terrier, the group rode on.

"That Holly Owen is a real pest!" Jo muttered
when Krista and Alice told her about the
incident in Mill Lane. "It's not the first time her
dog has been let loose to run at the ponies."

"'Let loose'? You mean, she did it on purpose?" Alice gasped.

Jo nodded. "The Owens think they rule the world. Mr Owen says we should keep the ponies away from his property, even though the lane is a public highway."

"Some people!" Krista sighed. She was still relieved that everyone was safe, and proud of Molly the heroine! Now she was ready to forget the whole thing.

Molly stood nearby, gently wagging her bushy tail.

"We're off now," Krista told Jo, going to fetch her bike from the side of the tack room. "I've put Shandy back in the field with the others. All the other jobs are done."

52

Sea Haze

"Thanks for everything," Jo replied. "See you tomorrow."

"Come on, Molly, time for supper. Lovely grub – yum-yum!" Krista called. She set off with a wave.

Alice and Jo watched them disappear into the lane. "She talks to the dog as if she understands every word!" Jo smiled. "Typical Krista!"

"This is the best view of Whitton Bay, and if you look behind us, you can see Black Point stretching out into the sea!" Krista stopped on the cliff path so that Molly could have a rest. The poor dog was panting and puffing as she tried to keep up.

My Magical Pony

Molly sat down, tongue hanging out, her sides heaving.

"This part of the path is special," Krista went on in a low voice, checking first to make sure that there was no one around. She laid her bike in the long grass and pointed to a nearby rock. "Don't tell anyone, Molly, but this is where I come to meet Shining Star. It's a magic spot!"

Molly cocked her head to one side and stared at the tall rock set in a sea of purple heather.

"It's a big, big secret!" Krista explained, walking closer to the rock. "Star made me promise never to tell anyone about him and his magic powers, but I know he wouldn't mind you

knowing. For a start, you can't tell anyone!"

Molly heaved a long sigh then settled her head on her front paws.

Carried away by memories of the adventures she'd had with her magical pony, Krista chatted on. "Shining Star is so amazing! He has wings and he can fly anywhere in the world. In fact, he flies here from Galishe, which you wouldn't know about, Moll, but it's a place millions of miles away. You have to fly amongst the stars to reach it, but Shining Star can do it easily because of his magic ..."

Molly snoozed as Krista talked.

"You know the most beautiful thing about him? He's pure white but he's covered in a kind of silver dust which sparkles and makes

him look as if he's glowing. And he's so kind and brave …" For once in her life, Krista could say what she felt. She turned her back on Molly to gaze up at the deep blue sky. "When he comes to see me, the first I know about it is a tiny cloud in the distance. It looks like a normal cloud at first, but if you look closely you can see that it shines silvery white and it travels towards you, getting bigger …"

Molly twitched her ears and opened her eyes. She'd heard a movement in the grass.

"… Then you have to wait until the cloud gets really close and it starts to sprinkle silver dust on to the ground …"

The noise was coming from underneath the wire fence, close to the edge of the cliff.

Sea Haze

Molly thought it might be a mouse or a weasel – something good to chase!

Krista wandered round the back of the rock, staring wistfully at the sky.

There was another rustle in the undergrowth. Molly crouched ready.

"… Finally you can see Shining Star inside the magic cloud. Usually it's his beautiful head and neck that take shape first …"

My Magical Pony

Woof! Molly pounced. She lost her footing and began to slide over the cliff edge. Pebbles came loose and fell to the beach below.

"Molly!" Krista yelled her name and came running from the magic spot, just in time to see the dog scrabbling to stay in sight.

Still the pebbles fell, rattling against the sheer cliff, showering down.

Krista flung herself to the ground and edged towards Molly, who had managed to keep her footing. Her back legs shook as she fought to climb back up. In a flash Krista grabbed her sturdy collar and hauled with all her might. It was enough – Molly made it back on to firm ground!

Chapter Four

"Poor Molly, it was all my fault!" Krista whispered as she plumped up the dog's bed that night. "I should have been watching what you were doing."

Her mum watched and listened. "Don't be too hard on yourself, love. You weren't to know that Molly would stray near the edge of the cliff."

"I should've been more careful." Krista stood aside to let Molly creep on to her bed. She stroked her softly. "Molly doesn't know her way around as well as I do. I should've been watching what she was doing."

My Magical Pony

"Hmm, Krista, what *were* you doing at the time?" her dad asked. He leaned against the doorway leading from the hallway into the kitchen, arms crossed, looking thoughtful.

Krista grimaced. She mustn't mention the magic spot or Shining Star. "Just daydreaming," she mumbled.

"Anyway, Molly's none the worse for wear," her mum concluded. "Not even a single scratch as far as I can see."

"Lucky!" her dad said. "If Molly were a cat I'd say she just used up one of her nine lives!"

"Don't joke about it," Krista begged, still stroking Molly's head.

"No, leave Krista alone. She's already feeling guilty enough," her mum agreed.

Sea Haze

She too bent down to give Molly a stroke. "Don't worry – in the morning, after a good night's sleep, it'll all be forgotten."

Krista nodded and made a brave attempt at a smile. But it came out crooked and tired. What would have happened if Molly had lost her footing and plummeted down the cliff? The poor dog would have died. Then what on earth would Krista have told Darcy when she came back from holiday?

Krista's mum took a long close look at her daughter's face. "Bedtime for you!" she said firmly. "And not up too early in the morning, please. You need to catch up on some sleep!"

*

61

My Magical Pony

Next morning dawned bright and sunny. The light filtered in through Krista's closed curtains, waking her before seven o'clock.

I wonder how Molly is! was her first thought.

Jumping out of bed, Krista dashed downstairs to find Molly yawning and beginning to stretch. When she saw Krista she wagged her tail then stiffly got to her feet. "Good girl," Krista murmured. "It's Monday today – the second week of the school holidays. How do you fancy another day at the stables?"

Wag-wag went Molly's tail.

"I take it that means 'yes'!" Krista smiled, going into the kitchen to give Molly a fresh drink and to grab a bowl of cereal for herself. "We can be at Hartfell by eight. Jo said I

62

could take Apollo into the
arena this morning and do
some dressage with him."

Wag-wag. Snuffle-slurp.

"That'll be fun," Krista
promised. "You can sit by
the arena fence and watch."

Molly finished her drink then
went eagerly to the back door.

Krista sighed and grinned. "Wait
there while I get dressed, Moll. You're lucky –
you've got a lovely silky coat, so you don't
have to bother with clothes!"

"Where's Misty's bridle? ... Fetch Shandy
and Drifter in from the field please, Krista ...

My Magical Pony

The vet rang to say he's dropping in at two to look at Woody's laminitis …" Busy as ever, Jo dashed here and there, asking Krista to run errands and letting her share what was going on at Hartfell.

Monday went, then Tuesday. Molly shadowed Krista wherever she went and by midweek everyone on the yard had grown used to having her around.

"That dog never lets you out of her sight," Alice commented early on Wednesday morning, as Molly nestled close to Krista while she took a break from mucking out.

Krista took a big swig of orange juice. "I know. I keep on getting e-mails from Darcy, asking me how Molly's doing. I e-mail back

Sea Haze

and tease her and say she's fine and not missing her one teensy-weensy bit!"

Jo came by, deep in conversation with John Carter, the vet.

"The problem is, once a pony's gone lame with laminitis in the past, it's likely to keep on happening, however careful you are," the vet was explaining. "Make sure you don't put Woody out to grass until he's sound again. And then only for an hour or so at a time."

Jo nodded. "You know he came from the Owens at the Old Mill?"

"Yes, I remember. That's when he first had the lameness problem," John said. "I visited him there."

My Magical Pony

The two grown-ups had stopped to talk outside the tack room door, unaware that Krista and Alice could overhear.

"Between you and me," Jo went on, "there's a chance that the Owens will want Woody back."

Krista's eyes widened in shock. She stared at Alice, who gasped.

"He came here on loan," Jo explained. "Holly Owen hadn't ridden him for six months and Mr Owen was glad to offload the pony on to me. But now apparently Holly has decided she wants to start riding again."

"No way!" Krista mouthed. She didn't dislike many people, but Holly Owen was definitely on the list. "She totally neglected Woody when she had him!"

66

Sea Haze

"Anyway, I thought Mr Owen didn't like horses," Alice whispered. "Doesn't he say they should stay off Mill Lane and not go near their house?"

Krista nodded and put her finger to her mouth. "Sshh!"

"I'd try to avoid letting him go back to the Owens," John Carter advised Jo.

"He's much better off with you here."

Jo agreed. "Maybe Mr Owen will see that. And maybe Holly will come to Hartfell to pick up riding again."

"Yuck!" Alice stuck a finger in her mouth and mimed being sick. "I so hate her!"

No one liked Holly Owen because she was bossy and stuck-up. And Holly had been especially mean to Alice when she'd first come down from Scotland.

Krista frowned. "Forget it," she said, thinking that no way would it happen. "Woody's fine here with us!"

The week sped by. On Friday morning, after Krista had brushed Molly and just before she

and Moll left for the stables, Krista went upstairs to get dressed and picked up another e-mail from Darcy.

Hi Krista, it said. **How's my Molly? Are you giving her enough to eat and making sure she gets lots of exercise? Having a great time here – went to Waterworld yesterday – dolphins were cool. Today we're going to see Snow White on Ice. Seriously, Krista, is Molly missing me? Luv, Darcy xxx.**

Krista e-mailed straight back. **Molly's doing great. Loves stables and ponies, especially Shandy. Don't worry, she's having cool time. And OK yes, she's missing you a teensy bit! See you soon. Luv, Krista xxx.**

She sat for a moment, gazing at the monitor

before she sent the message. *We're almost halfway through the two weeks,* she thought with a pang of regret. *Only eight more days, not counting today, before Molly has to go home!*

Pulling herself together, she went downstairs and into the kitchen to put on her riding boots. "Here, Moll!" she called.

It looked like the dog had pushed open the back door and gone for a wander in the yard.

Krista eased the boots on. "Come here, Molly!" she called again. She went outside. The yard was empty except for a pair of grey wood pigeons pecking at the seed which Krista's mum had thrown down the night before. Krista frowned and went back into the house.

She checked the kitchen and hallway, went

into the lounge then dashed upstairs. *This is weird!* she thought. Molly had never gone walkabout before.

Krista retraced her steps out into the yard. She called Molly's name, louder this time. Still nothing.

"Everything OK?" her dad asked, poking his head out of the bedroom window.

"I can't find Molly," Krista told him, running around the side of the house to search the front garden. She looked under the bench, amongst the flowering bushes and under the hawthorn hedge, her heat beating fast.

"Spike, have you seen Molly?" she gasped, spotting the little hedgehog rummaging underneath the bushes.

My Magical Pony

Of course Spike didn't pay her any attention. Instead, he scratched with his sharp front claws at the soft earth, looking for worms and grubs.

By now Krista was in a panic. She stood at the garden gate, looking out at the heathery hillside, desperate to spot the runaway dog. "Molly!" she yelled, her hands cupped around her mouth.

Molly – Molly – Molly! A faint echo came back from the empty hills.

Chapter Five

"It's OK, she can't have gone far!" Krista's dad said as he ran out into the garden. He'd heard Krista's frantic calls, got dressed and come as quickly as he could.

"But Molly never wanders off!" Krista wailed. Suddenly the bottom seemed to have dropped out of her perfect world.

Her dad put his arm around her shoulder. "I expect she got on the scent of something interesting. She'll follow it for a bit, then she'll be back here, tail between her legs, you'll see."

My Magical Pony

Nodding and sniffing, Krista let herself be led back to the house, where her mum was up and dressed. "Mum, Molly's gone missing. What do we do?"

"Wait for a while," her mum advised, though she looked anxiously around the yard.

"We can't just stand here!" Krista pleaded. The minutes were ticking by. "What if she's gone along the cliff path? You know what happened earlier this week at the magi— I mean ... at the edge of the cliff!" A careless slip of the tongue almost gave away Shining Star's secret.

"What do you think?" her mum asked her dad.

"Hmm, maybe one of us should stay here,

Sea Haze

while the other drives Krista around the area to take a look."

The plan was quickly agreed, so while Krista's mum stayed at High Point, Krista and her dad jumped in the car. They edged out into the lane, trying to decide which way Molly was most likely to have gone.

"Let's try the places she already knows," Krista's dad suggested.

Krista sat silent in the passenger seat. *What am I going to tell Darcy?* she thought over and over. Her heart thudded dully, her stomach felt empty and hollow.

"Wind down the window and call her," Krista's dad said, driving down the narrow lane towards town. "Your mum is going to call the

neighbours to ask them to keep a lookout."

"What if she went up on to the moor? We might be going the wrong way," Krista murmured.

"We can't drive in every direction at once."

"But what if she's on one of these twisty lanes and a car comes round a bend and she gets run over?"

"Try not to think about it. Go on, yell her name."

"Molly!" Krista cried, leaning her head out of the window so the wind whipped her hair from her face.

Sea Haze

"OK, I'm going to turn off and head for Hartfell," her dad decided when they came to a junction in the road. "The most likely thing is that, if she got lost, she would head for the place she knows best, next to High Point."

Krista nodded. She kept on calling Molly's name as once more the car climbed the hill and cut across to the stables. *Please be there!* she begged silently, closing her eyes and wishing as hard as she could.

By the time her dad drove into the stable yard, Krista had convinced herself that Molly would be sitting under the tack room porch waiting for them. She would see their car, woof and trot to meet them, pleading with her dark brown eyes for them not to be cross.

My Magical Pony

Please! Krista begged silently, closing her eyes and not daring to look.

Krista's dad looked around the busy scene then shook his head. "No sign of Molly," he muttered.

Krista opened her eyes. She saw Alice and Nathan busy with the ponies, plus the unwelcome sight of Holly Owen and her mother talking to Jo. But Molly was nowhere to be seen. She sighed, burying her head in her hands.

"Come on. Let's at least put out a missing-dog alert." Sighing too, Krista's dad got out of the car. He went to talk to Alice first.

Slowly Krista walked over to Jo. She felt Holly ignore her, but if she was honest she

didn't care. All that mattered was to pass on the message about Molly.

"So, Holly definitely wants to ride Woody again," Mrs Owen was saying to Jo. "We're thinking we'd like to have him back at the Old Mill for the rest of the summer holidays."

"Hmm, he's still getting over a touch of laminitis," Jo told them. "And besides, he's used to having other ponies around now. He might be lonely if he came back to you."

Mrs Owen tutted and Holly tossed her head as if to say that no one could tell her anything she didn't know.

"Why not come and ride him here?" Jo suggested.

"No way!" Holly cried. "I want him back!"

My Magical Pony

Her mum seemed less sure. "Maybe that's a good idea," she cut in. "At least we wouldn't have all the hard work of looking after Woody. And besides, it would keep your dad happy. He doesn't really want Woody back with us."

"Dad's just being mean!" Holly wailed. "Woody's still my pony, and I want him!"

By this time Krista had heard enough. She stepped between the Owens and Jo. "Molly's gone missing," she told her quickly. "You haven't seen her, have you?"

After that, everyone flew around the yard searching in corners, inside the tack room, even in Jo's house overlooking the stables, where her two cats sat undisturbed. Still no Molly.

Sea Haze

"OK, I suggest we spread the search." Jo took charge, hastily saying goodbye to the Owens. "Let's tack up the ponies and ride out in different directions."

Everyone was eager to follow the new plan. Alice saddled Nessie then helped Krista fasten Shandy's girth.

"I'm so clumsy!" Krista muttered as the broad strap slid from her grasp. She knew that Shandy could tell how upset she was by the way she shifted uneasily and tugged at her lead-rope.

"Good girl!" Alice whispered, soothing the pony. Soon both she and Krista were ready to ride.

"OK, I'll drive on and keep looking,"

My Magical Pony

Krista's dad told them. "I'm going to try the Stevens' place in town, just in case Molly wandered back home. Jo and Nathan are heading for the moor top. Why don't you and Alice try the beach?"

As Krista put her foot in the stirrup and mounted Shandy, Mrs Owen backed her car out of the yard. She came too close to Shandy and the pony shied away. Just in time, Krista settled in the saddle. "Whoa!" she said, noticing Holly give her the evil eye before her mum finally drove off. *What did I do?* she wondered.

In any case, there was no time to dwell on it. Everyone was leaving the yard, calling and telling Krista not to worry, that they were sure that Molly would soon turn up.

Sea Haze

Alice and Krista set off along the cliff path
towards the bridleway that led down to
Whitton Sands. The sudden quiet struck them
after the bustle of the stables, and the huge,
open space that the searchers had to cover.
Krista gazed ahead then down below to the
curve of the bay. She saw white clouds low over
the horizon. "Oh, how are we ever going to
find her?" she asked.

My Magical Pony

"I don't know, but we will!" Alice squeezed Nessie into action, going ahead down the steep bridleway leading to the beach. "Molly knows her way around. And she's a sensible dog. I'm sure she can take care of herself."

"Unless she's been hurt," Krista pointed out. "What if she's injured or ... worse?"

"Stop!" Alice said with a shudder. She waited for Krista and Shandy to join her on the beach. Then she turned to yell Molly's name along the sands.

"That's a sea mist," Krista muttered, watching the low clouds roll in towards them. This was all they needed!

They rode on, close to the edge of the beach where the cliff rose sheer above their

84

heads. The two ponies trod carefully over the smooth pebbles, their hooves clattering.

"What's that?" Alice pointed to a pale shape lying on the ground, half hidden behind a rock.

Krista's heart missed a beat. She dismounted and ran to the spot. "It's only an old sack!" she called. The dirty plastic sack was caught on a piece of driftwood, tangled up in seaweed and other rubbish.

Alice nodded, waiting for Krista to remount. She peered up at the dark cliff. "You know, I actually hope we don't find anything down here!" she admitted.

Krista nodded. "Wouldn't it be awful if ..." Unable to finish the sentence, she patted

My Magical Pony

Shandy's sturdy neck and urged her on.

In the distance, the waves rolled on to the shore with a muffled sound. The sea haze thickened and curled its way towards the two riders.

Sea Haze

"What's that under the ledge?" Krista said. This time she stayed in the saddle as she drew near.

"It looks like a big chunk from a tree," Alice decided, peering through the wet mist.

Sure enough, the object under the ledge was part of a trunk, stripped of its bark, its branches chopped off and its surface smoothed by the waves. Krista frowned and turned away. "Molly!" she yelled, feeling cold and hopeless.

Alice shook her head. "Look at this mist. It's dangerous. We'd better get out of here."

By now the haze had completely surrounded them, turning the warm air chilly. "We'll never find anything anyway," Krista agreed, setting Shandy back the way they'd come.

My Magical Pony

The ponies trudged slowly over the pebbles, heads down, ears flicking anxiously this way and that. The girls' spirits were low, and they rode in silence.

"Nothing," Jo reported, back at Hartfell.

"Nothing," Krista's dad echoed. "I went to the Stevens' house and Molly wasn't there."

The cold mist swirled around the stable yard. For now the search had to be called off.

"At least until this sea haze lifts," Jo said firmly. "I can't risk the ponies being out in this weather."

Krista hung her head. She didn't want to give up. She wanted to keep on looking. "Poor Molly!" she groaned.

Sea Haze

Alice knew what she was going through.
"I know, it's a real shame," she said quietly.

They all stood sadly in the yard until
Krista's dad made the first move. "Let's go
home," he told Krista, opening the car door
and bundling her inside.

"No!" she protested.

"Yes." Jo agreed with her dad. She
squeezed Krista's shoulder then closed the car
door. "All we can do now is wait!"

Chapter Six

The sea mist clothed everything in a dull, damp blanket. It had rolled in with the tide, creeping up the hillsides and over the top of Hartfell Moor.

On the journey home Krista sat in silence beside her dad. She thought of Molly wandering lost on the moor or lying hurt in a rocky inlet in Whitton Bay. Eventually though her mind went numb and she stared emptily into the thick mist swirling into the car's fog lights.

"Come inside!" Krista's mum greeted them with mugs of hot chocolate. She could tell by

the looks on their faces that there was still no sign of the missing dog.

"We've looked everywhere!" Krista told her, slumping on to a chair at the kitchen table.

Her mum nodded. "I tried the RSPCA centre, to see if anyone had found Molly and taken her there. But, no luck!"

"It's like she vanished into thin air," Krista sighed, remembering again the moment when she'd left Molly waiting by the kitchen door while she dashed upstairs to get dressed. It already seemed an age ago, she thought wearily.

Krista's dad sipped his chocolate. "Don't give up hope," he said. "You hear stories of dogs disappearing for weeks and then suddenly turning up again out of the blue."

91

My Magical Pony

Krista groaned. "Darcy comes back at the end of next week. What am I going to tell her if Molly's still missing?"

"Talk about putting your foot in it!" her mum muttered to her dad, as Krista burst into tears and dashed from the room.

Upstairs, she sat down at her desk, mopping up the tears with a tissue. As luck would

have it, the screen on her e-mail system showed she had a new message from Darcy. Without thinking, Krista clicked her mouse.

Sea Haze

Hi Krista. Didn't go to ice show after all. Mum feeling faint in the heat. Thought I'd e-mail to ask about Molly again. Really and truly this time, how much is she missing me? More than a teensy bit, I hope!!
Luv, Darcy xxx

Krista gulped and quickly clicked the mouse to log off. No way did she want to send an answer right now. But the message hit home. It made Krista jump up and pace the room, turning as she reached the bed and striding back towards the window.

Go away, mist! she said to herself. *Blow over – disappear – whoosh!*

She walked round her room again, unable to sit still. *I have to do something!* she thought.

My Magical Pony

Round and round, growing more desperate,
Krista kept returning to the window. The fog
was still thick, the world grey and silent.

"Of course!" It came to her at last and she
spoke out loud. "Shining Star!"

Krista's mum and dad were watching TV in the
lounge when Krista slipped from the house.

She ran across the yard without glancing
back, past the parked car and through the
gate on to the lane. Within seconds she was
climbing over the stile on to the cliff path.

Then she found she had to slow down.
It was dangerous to run now that the ground
was uneven and she could scarcely see two
metres in front of her. "Weird!" she muttered,

reaching out a hand to feel the rough fence post on her right. "This mist is so thick I can hardly see where I'm going!"

Luckily, though she couldn't see the edge of the cliff she knew that by following the fence posts she could stick to the rough track. "Slowly!" she breathed, carefully putting one foot after another, one step at a time. A move in the wrong direction in this strange white world could send her crashing over the cliff.

The journey to the magic spot seemed to take forever. Krista felt her way, longing for the tall rock to appear out of the mist, fearing in the end that she had somehow walked past it without realising. But no – there was a

crooked fence post and a dip in the barbed
wire which she recognised, and after that a
slight hill, and then the rock looming out of
the mist.

Thank goodness! Krista walked right up to
the boulder and touched its rough surface.
Now all she had to do was to call for her
magical pony.

"Shining Star, it's me – Krista!" Her soft
voice was muffled by the mist. What if he
couldn't hear or see her? What then? She
spoke up now, calling his name a second time,
gazing through the fog. "I'm at the magic
spot. I need your help!"

Krista seemed to wait a long time but there
was no response.

96

Sea Haze

"Oh please come!" she cried. She kept one hand flat against the rock to steady herself, looking in vain for the magical pony's silver cloud.

No, he hadn't heard her. The sea haze had deadened her voice and made her invisible from far-off Galishe.

Krista's shoulders sagged and she turned to go. But there, in front of her, not five metres away was a dusting of glittery silver on the grass and Shining Star standing quietly, watching and waiting.

In an instant Krista's spirits lifted. She ran to meet the glowing, pure white figure whose wings rested quietly by his sides, whose dark eyes were fixed intently on her.

97

Sea Haze

"I'd almost given up!" she whispered.

"Never lose hope," Shining Star told her. "Though I am far away, I always hear you call."

"But the mist …" Krista said, stepping on the glittering grass. Yet she should have known that Star could fly anywhere, through time and space, during night or day, whatever the weather. "I'm so pleased to see you!"

Shining Star nodded. "Why do you need me? Have the wild ponies been trapped at Black Point again?"

"No, it's not the ponies this time. It's Molly!" Krista began to explain rapidly about how Molly had been living with them at High Point and how she'd suddenly gone missing at breakfast time that morning.

99

My Magical Pony

Shining Star put his head to one side. He looked puzzled. "Did Molly say anything before she left?"

Krista stared back at him. "Oh no, didn't I tell you? Molly's a dog!"

"Ah!" the magical pony understood.

"A gorgeous, soft, silky golden retriever with enormous brown eyes—"

"Who has disappeared." Star cut in as if there was no time to lose. "Have you searched for her already?"

Krista nodded. "We've looked everywhere – on the lanes, in town, at the stables. No one knows where she is. In the end I knew I had to come to you and ask you to help."

"And I will," Star assured her. "But you must

100

speak more slowly and tell me about the
moment when your friend Molly disappeared.
Climb on my back and you can talk as we go."

Willingly Krista did as she was told. She
sat astride the pony's broad back, holding on
to his shiny mane, her legs tucked behind his
wings, feeling the sway of his body as he
began to walk.

"Molly was sitting there, good as gold by
the kitchen door at home," Krista explained.
"I dashed upstairs to get ready to go to the
stables. When I came back down, she'd gone!"

"You didn't hear her bark, or any other
noise before she disappeared?"

"No. It was early. No one came to the
house. Mum and Dad were still asleep."

Shining Star walked on through the mist without fear. "I think we must return to High Point," he decided.

"But … What … Oh no … Oh yeah!" *But,* she thought, *what if Mum and Dad catch sight of us? Oh no, of course. If they see us, you'll just look to them like any other little grey pony wandering on the moors. Oh yeah!* "Good idea!" she agreed.

"We will return to High Point and pick up Molly's trail," Shining Star explained, stepping out more quickly. "It is not safe for a dog to be lost when the sea covers the world in mist. It is worse than dark nights when winds howl through the trees, worse than snow in winter driving against the hills. Come, let us hurry."

Chapter Seven

Krista's mum and dad looked anxiously out of the kitchen window.

"You're sure Krista's not in her room?" her dad asked.

Her mum shook her head. "No, she must have slipped out. I do hope she didn't go far."

They waited a while, wondering what on earth Krista was up to now. Then her dad spotted a faint shape in the lane and heard the muffled sound of a horse's hooves. He went out into the yard.

Krista rode Shining Star bareback.

My Magical Pony

He came to help! she thought, gathering courage now that Star was here and the sea mist was beginning to clear. She saw her dad waiting for her in the yard.

"Krista, you know you're not supposed to slip out of the house without telling us!" he cried, seeing that she seemed to have teamed up with one of the wild moorland ponies. "You had us really worried!"

"Sorry," she murmured, easing herself down to the ground and holding on to Star's thick mane.

Krista's mum joined them. "Thank goodness!" she said. She stared at the shaggy grey pony. "Wherever did you find him?"

Krista wanted to get on with searching for

Sea Haze

Molly. She could feel the air clearing, the sun beginning to burn off the mist. "He was wandering in the lane."

"He seems very tame," her mum said. "Is this the pony you've made friends with before?"

Hurriedly Krista nodded. "He lets me ride him. I thought he could help me look for Molly."

"Yes well, it's good that the fog is clearing." Her dad stepped in with fresh plans. "I think it's worth me driving out for another scout around."

Krista's mum agreed. "I'll get on the phone again – let people know we're still looking."

"I'll search the garden one more time," Krista told them, leading Star round the side of the house where the mist had risen from the lawn but still lingered in the trees and hedges.

He walked quietly, though his ears were pricked and he was alert. "I smell the scent of the dog," he told Krista. "It is in the air."

"Does that mean she's close by?" Krista's heartbeat quickened.

"No, it is an old scent. But I smell other creatures – birds in their nests, hedgehogs in the long grass …"

"That must be Spike!" Krista cried. She ran to his nest-box close to the hawthorn hedge.

Shining Star came and nosed against Spike's box. "Now there is the scent of freshly dug earth," he said thoughtfully. He turned his attention to the ground under the hedge. "Here is a hole, and it is deep."

Krista fell to her knees to see the big patch

of bare earth. A closer look showed her large
paw marks imprinted in the soil.

"That is the fresh track of a dog," Star
decided, raising his head and gazing around
the garden.

Krista nodded and thought things through.
No way was this hole here yesterday when
she'd come to feed Spike. So it must have been
dug that morning, which meant that Molly
must have grown bored waiting for Krista and
come into the garden for a root around.

My Magical Pony

Unluckily for her, she'd chosen to snuffle and dig right on Spike's patch. And, as Krista already knew, hedgehogs and dogs didn't always get on! "I think Spike and Molly had a fight!" she cried. "They did the same thing when Molly first arrived!"

It was Shining Star's turn to nod. "Look, here is pale golden fur caught on the thorns of the hedge. Your friend Molly squeezed under here to get away!"

Krista touched the strands of soft hair. They had found a clue. Now she was sure that this was what had happened. "OK, so Molly squeezed under the hedge and ran away! But which way did she go? Why didn't she come back?"

Sea Haze

"We will follow her trail," Shining Star decided, telling Krista to climb on his back. He waited until she was safely mounted then quickly spread his wings. "Many hours have passed," he reminded her. "But there will be paw prints and perhaps other signs."

Krista felt her magical pony rise from the grass. She held tight to his mane as they cleared the hedge and began to circle the field beyond.

Shining Star flew close to the ground, which seemed to tilt. Only, Krista knew it was Star who was leaning this way and that, skimming as close as he dared to the grass and hedges. The thrill of sailing through the air gripped her. "Oh!" she cried, as Star

beat his wings to clear a hedge, then swerved
to fly around a post pointing the way to
Whitton. "You're going too fast. I can't see a
thing!"

"But I can," Star told her calmly. "There were
prints in the mud by the water trough in the
first field, and now I am following a track across
the lane into the ploughed field beyond."

Glancing round, Krista saw that Shining
Star was heading downhill, but not towards
the town. They were flying over farmland,
with the cliffs and the sea to their right, the
high moors to their left. He still skimmed the
ground in his search, hovering every now and
then to study marks in soft mud, then turning
to follow another trail.

110

Sea Haze

"That's the Bellwoods' place!" Krista pointed out a smart converted farmhouse. "I know exactly where we are!"

Star flew on more slowly, past the ploughed field and the farm, across grassland where sheep grazed. "The trail is difficult now," he explained.

Below was a narrow lane between two fields. Trees lined the roadside, casting long shadows.

My Magical Pony

Krista recognised one old oak tree by its weird, twisted trunk, then spotted the entrance to a bridleway marked with a signpost. "This is Mill Lane. Do you think Molly got this far?"

Shining Star beat his wings gently, hovering on the spot. "The dog was here," he decided. "But now there is a question in my mind – she was here, on this spot, but then something happened."

"What?" Krista grew alarmed. She wanted to know what her magical pony could see in his mind's eye.

"There was fog," he told her. "It gathered in this hollow. There is a sound of running water. Then there is darkness."

Sea Haze

"What kind of darkness?"

The magical pony shook his head. "An empty room without windows. I cannot tell you more."

Krista's forehead creased in a deep frown. "The only house around here is the Old Mill, where Holly Owen lives with her mum and dad."

Shining Star nodded. "Does it stand by water?"

"Yes, there's the old mill race – a kind of rushing waterfall, and a pond with a big old wooden wheel that they used for power to turn the millstones." Krista had seen it once a few years earlier, when she'd visited the empty house with her mum and dad.

My Magical Pony

They'd even thought of buying it, but the Owens had put in a higher offer.

"We must search for Molly at this house," Star decided. He landed in the lane and waited for Krista to dismount before he folded his wings.

Still Krista frowned. "If only it was somebody else's house!" she muttered, reluctantly following Star along the lane. She didn't fancy facing Holly Owen or her dog, Buster, and asking if they could take a look around.

"Come!" the magical pony said, puzzled by Krista's unhappy face. He began to trot, forcing her to run alongside. Soon the house came into view.

The Old Mill was a tall, stone building with

small windows. A stream ran to one side, where an ancient wooden wheel stood as a reminder of past times. To the other side was a range of low buildings, including a smart stable and a small barn.

"Can you see anything?" Krista gasped, out of breath from running to keep up.

"Only the dark room," Star replied, not looking at the house, but gazing skywards. "There are secrets here, and anger and fear."

Krista sighed. "Oh and look, here comes Holly!"

Sure enough, a figure came out of the gate into the lane. Holly recognised Krista and came marching towards her and the shaggy grey moorland pony. "Is that the best you can do?" she scoffed.

"What?"

"This scruffy little thing!" Holly jabbed her finger towards Star. "What happened? Won't Jo Weston let you ride her ponies any more?"

Krista ignored her. *If only she knew!* she thought. "Listen, Holly, we're still looking

Sea Haze

for Molly. You know, you were at the stables earlier on ..."

"Yeah, yeah. You went and lost Darcy's dog!" Holly sneered. "That's just like you to do something stupid! So what are you doing snooping around here?"

"We ... erm ... I followed some tracks. They belong to Molly, and we ... I ... think she came this way!"

Holly jutted out her chin and put her hands on her hips. "She's not here!"

Shining Star tossed his head and stared at the house and its beautifully kept garden.

"Are you sure?" Krista pleaded. "Could we please take a look?"

"Yes, I'm sure. And no you can't!" Holly snapped back.

Star shifted restlessly from foot to foot. He skittered sideways when a car door banged and an engine started.

"Hey!" Holly yelled at Krista. "Can't you make that pony behave?"

"Look, Holly, I don't know why you're being like this with me, but you must know how important it is for me to find Molly!" Krista could see that Holly wouldn't back down and she was growing desperate. "All we want to do is take a look!"

"No way!" As her father's car turned into

the lane and came speedily towards them, Holly tucked herself against the hedge.

The car screeched to a halt. Mr Owen leaned out of the window, his dog Buster yapping at his elbow. "Get that pony off the lane!" he yelled at Krista. "Can't you see it's blocking my way?"

Scared by the roaring engine and the smell of exhaust fumes, Star backed down the lane until he came to the bridleway.

119

My Magical Pony

He reared as he turned into the narrow track, his tail swishing against the side of Mr Owen's car.

Krista ran after Shining Star. "Are you OK?"

Star nodded. "The anger is the man's. The fear belongs to the girl," he told her.

"Huh!" Krista had never thought of Holly Owen as frightened. Only stuck-up and sneaky. She glanced down the lane to see that Holly had vanished into her house. "What now?" she asked.

Star listened and looked. "I see a dark room, I hear a dog whimpering," he told Krista, his voice serious and determined. "The girl was lying. The dog is here."

Chapter Eight

"If Holly won't let us look, we'll have to sneak in!" Krista decided.

Star agreed. "Let us wait until the car is far away."

They stood on the bridleway, looking up at a clear sky until the sound of the engine had died. Now all they could hear were the songs of the birds in the trees and the distant racing of the mill stream.

"OK?" Krista asked.

At last Star decided the time was right for Krista to mount and for them to creep forward.

My Magical Pony

Star kept to the grass verge so that his hooves didn't ring out on the road. They soon came to the gate and looked around the empty yard.

Krista saw a garage with an open door and a car inside. There were tubs of flowers everywhere, a horse trailer parked close to the old mill wheel, mown lawns to each side of the snaking stream. The door to the house was open, the sound of music drifting through it.

"Dare we go closer?" Krista murmured to Star, glad that there was no chance of the terrier overhearing.

"Search in the barn while I wait here," he whispered back.

Quickly Krista dismounted and edged around the side of the garden furthest

122

away from the house. She darted from
bush to bush until she came to the door of
the barn.

This sure is a dark room! she said to herself,
peering inside. The long barn was stacked
with old furniture and boxes, bikes, a broken
garden swing. "Molly?" Krista whispered.

There was no reply. The only sound Krista
could hear was her own heart beating. She
inched forward, feeling her way.

"N-O – No!" a woman's voice said, out in
the yard.

Krista gasped and crouched down behind
the garden swing.

"But Mum!" This was Holly, following her
mother out into the yard.

123

My Magical Pony

"I'm afraid the answer is no," Mrs Owen repeated. "You heard what your father said. There is absolutely no way that he will allow you to have Woody back here with us!"

"But why not?" Holly sounded close to tears.

"It's not up to me, darling. Dad says you don't deserve it. He wants you to do better with your school work before he'll even consider it."

There was a pause as Mrs Owen walked across the yard towards the garage. Holly followed her. "Dad's always telling me off and

blaming me for stuff," she complained. "Sometimes I don't even know what I did wrong!"

"Well, that's how he is, and all we can do is keep out of his way when he's in this mood," came the reply. "And I do see his point about Woody – you never kept up your side of the deal to look after him properly when he did live here!"

"But I will now!" Holly pleaded. "Mum, you have to make Dad change his mind!"

Listening from the barn, Krista pictured how Holly must be stopping her mum from getting into her car and driving off.

"You know I can't do that," she sighed. "You realise your dad *never* changes his mind."

125

"But what if I did something really good?"
Holly begged.

"Like what?"

"Like – I don't know – cleaning my room!"

Mrs Owen tutted. "It'll take more than
that, Holly."

"OK, like – saving someone's life!"

Holly's mum laughed. "Don't be silly, dear."

"Well – OK then – like finding that dog!"

Krista gasped and strained to listen.

"The dog that's gone missing from Krista's
house," Holly reminded her mum. "You
know – we heard about it this morning. If I
managed to find her, Dad would be really
pleased with me, wouldn't he?"

There was another long pause.

Sea Haze

"He likes dogs, even if he doesn't like horses!" Holly pointed out.

Mrs Owen came out with another strained laugh. "Please be sensible, Holly. Sometimes I think you live in a dream world, not the real world at all!"

I'm not so sure! Krista thought grimly. Suddenly a lot of things were beginning to slot into place. Like, for instance, why Holly had refused to let Krista look around the Old Mill!

"I want Dad to let me have Woody back!" Holly tailed off feebly as her mum got into her car and started the engine. "I'd do anything!"

These were the last words Krista heard before Mrs Owen backed out of the garage and drove off.

127

Krista waited. She heard Holly's footsteps cross the yard and peeped out. Holly was crying and begging for her mum to stop and listen, but the car disappeared down the lane.

"What are you staring at?" Holly yelled at Shining Star, who still stood by the gate. "What are you even doing here?"

Star lowered his head and turned towards Krista. Holly spun round.

"Sneak!" she yelled when she saw Krista. "You come out of that barn, or I'll … I'll …"

"You'll what?" Krista asked, suddenly calm. She'd heard enough from Holly to realise exactly what she was up to. "Listen, you have to tell me what you've done with Molly!"

Shining Star gazed intently at the guilty,

frightened girl. Krista could see that he was breathing a beautiful shimmering mist over her, surrounding her with a bright halo of glittering light.

"I haven't done … anything … with your stupid … dog!" Holly's voice trailed off.

She seemed confused and still close to tears.

Star's light glowed softly. He stared into Holly's eyes.

"It's OK, you can trust us," Krista murmured, approaching Holly. "How are you feeling? Are you OK?"

Holly shook her head and let the tears run down her cheeks. "I feel kind of weird. I don't know why I'm talking to you. This isn't supposed to happen."

"What *is* supposed to happen?"

"I'm meant to keep Molly hidden until everyone's given up looking. Then I 'find' her, and she's safe, and everyone thinks how great I am, and it's cool, and even Dad says he's pleased with me ..." Once more Holly trailed off.

Sea Haze

Krista glanced at Shining Star and smiled. His magical cloud had brought them to the truth of what had happened. "So where did you hide Molly?" she asked Holly.

Holly shook her head. "I can't … I mean … I …"

The magical pony came up and nudged her gently.

"OK, I found her wandering down the lane about two hours ago. I put her on a lead and hid her in the horse trailer," Holly confessed, hanging her head and crying quietly.

"A dark room without a window!" Krista said to Shining Star. She'd thought of a barn, and perhaps a cellar, but never about a trailer! She ran across the yard towards it.

131

My Magical Pony

There was a narrow side door in the trailer which was bolted and padlocked. Krista ran round to the back, almost losing her footing and sliding down the slope towards the water wheel. She regained her balance then began to tug at the bolt fastening the ramp in place. "It's OK, Molly, I'm going to let you out!" she called.

At the sound of her voice there was a loud whimper from inside the trailer and a scratching of paws against the metal doors.

"You poor thing!" Krista muttered, struggling with the bolt.

Molly yelped and whined, scrabbling to be let out.

Holly ran across to help. "Let me do it,"

she said, taking Krista's place. "The bolt is stiff. You have to wiggle it loose."

A few seconds later the bolt slid back and the ramp dropped down. Molly rushed out, covered in straw from the floor of the trailer, scared by the dark and shaking all over.

Holly ducked out of the way of the falling ramp and knocked into Krista. Both girls lost their balance and slid towards the deep mill pond. Molly hurtled past them, straight into the water.

Krista yelled out. Star trotted swiftly across the yard. Krista saw Molly plunge in and vanish under the surface, then without thinking, she stumbled in after her.

The water was cold and very deep.

My Magical Pony

Weeds pulled at Krista's legs as she waded out of her depth then struggled to stay afloat. Across the pond she saw Molly's pale head come up to the surface. Behind her, the pond narrowed into a stream which tumbled over a sheer drop into the mill race. "Watch out, Molly!" Krista yelled, as the dog was dragged by the current towards the wide, crashing waterfall.

134

Sea Haze

From the grassy bank Holly cried for Krista to come back.

Krista kicked free of the weeds, and for a moment she reached up and clung to the rim of the great wooden wheel. It creaked and turned, plunging her back into the water. By now Molly was being swept along by the current, faster and faster into danger. In a few seconds she would disappear over the edge into the swirling waters below.

But Shining Star flew swiftly to save her, swooping low over the water, casting a sparkling shadow over Molly's head. At the last moment, on the very edge of the roaring water, Star folded his wings and plunged in beside the struggling dog.

My Magical Pony

A second later Molly had clambered across the pony's back and Star was swimming strongly for the bank.

Krista took a deep breath and swam towards Holly.

"How did …?" Holly stared in amazement as Shining Star carried Molly out of the water. "How did the pony do that?"

"Don't ask!" Krista spluttered, struggling up the muddy slope on to the lawn.

Holly helped her out of the water. "No but, how …?"

Krista knew that only she could see Star's magic. "It's a mystery!" she gasped, shivering and dripping at the water's edge.

Chapter Nine

Hi Darcy, Krista e-mailed her friend in Florida, **Sorry I didn't write back earlier – was busy. Molly is cool. And OK, yeah, she's missing you more than a teensy bit! Luv, Krista xxx**

She wrote as soon as she got home, after Shining Star had rescued Molly from the water and Holly's mum had arrived back home in her car. Mrs Owen had rushed out with towels for them all, fussing and anxious, glad that everyone was safe.

"Thanks to Holly," Krista had said.

My Magical Pony

Holly had gasped, stared at Krista then bitten her lip.

"How do you mean, 'thanks to Holly'?" her mum had asked.

Krista had glanced at Shining Star then said, "Holly was the one who found Molly in the first place. The pony and me – we just happened to be nearby."

Mrs Owen had hugged her daughter. "Are you OK?" she'd asked. "You didn't do anything silly?"

Holly had shaken her head. "No. Molly fell in the water by accident. We all helped drag her out."

Mrs Owen had believed them. She'd fussed over everyone and made sure no one was hurt.

Sea Haze

Star had waited patiently in the yard while Molly, Krista and Holly were towelled dry. He'd walked back to High Point with Krista and Molly.

And now he was in the garden with Molly and Spike while Krista sent her message to Darcy.

Once she'd finished, she dashed downstairs.

"Looks like that little grey pony is becoming a fixture around here!" her dad remarked as Krista whizzed through the kitchen.

"Yeah, he's cute," Krista grinned.

"She must have a way with the wild ponies as well as the ones at Hartfell," her mum added, watching their daughter run out on to

the lawn to join the animals. "This little one is unbelievably tame."

"She's got the magic touch," Krista's dad agreed.

Molly bounded up to Krista and wagged her tail. Her soft coat was dry and silky, her eyes bright.

Krista hugged and stroked her. She sat on the grass between Spike and Molly. "You two must stop arguing!" she warned sternly. "You hear? No more fights!"

Spike snuffled noisily at her feet while Molly kept a safe distance.

"That's better!" Krista smiled. She looked up at Shining Star, knowing that it was time

for him to fly home to Galishe.

Star gazed down at her, spreading his great wings and scattering his silver dust. "There is still a surprise in store for you," he promised quietly.

"For me?" Krista felt she'd had all the surprises she needed for one day.

My Magical Pony

"Tomorrow," Star predicted. "When the sun has gone down on this misty day and rises again in a clear sky. You will go to Hartfell as usual?"

Krista nodded.

"Holly will come too. She will ride her little brown pony."

"Are you sure?" Krista thought hard and saw how it might happen – Holly's dad would get to hear about her good deed in rescuing Molly, he would soften a bit and say OK, she could start riding again. But Woody couldn't come back to the Old Mill, Mr Owen would insist. She would have to ride him at Hartfell – he must stay there with the other ponies. A wiser Holly would agree.

Sea Haze

"OK, cool," Krista told Shining Star.

"The fear has gone from her eyes," Star said, looking into the future. "She is happy now."

"Me too!" Krista grinned. "Happy about Holly getting to ride again. Happy that Molly is safe!"

"You have a warm heart," Shining Star told her. He beat his wings and rose from the ground.

Krista felt the breeze from Star's wings on her face. She kept one arm around Molly and watched as he flew high in the sky.

Molly licked her hand.

Shining Star rose, surrounded by a bright mist.

143

My Magical Pony

"Goodbye!" Krista whispered.

Her dad glanced out of the window and saw Krista gazing at the empty sky. "Huh, where did the wild pony go?" he wondered to himself.

Krista hugged Molly, who wagged her tail. They looked deep into each other's eyes. "Hey, we get to hang out together for one more whole week!" Krista said with the widest of smiles.